ONCE UPON A FARM

Muriel Kingsley

ARTHUR H. STOCKWELL LTD
Torrs Park, Ilfracombe, Devon, EX34 8BA
Established 1898
www.ahstockwell.co.uk

British Library Cataloguing-in-Publication Data.
A catalogue record for this book is available
from the British Library.

By the same author:
Two Little Mice and Mary-Ann
Mary-Ann's Grandma's Ghost Story
Emily's Great Adventure
The Widow and the Vicar

ISBN 978-0-7223-5117-8
Printed in Great Britain by
Arthur H. Stockwell Ltd
Torrs Park   Ilfracombe
Devon EX34 8BA

Once upon a time, on the beautiful island of Jamaica, the trees and grass were always green and the rivers and gullies ran fast. On the top of the hill there lived a young farmer. His name was Daniel. He lived with Angela, his beautiful wife, and their seven-year-old bouncy magical daughter, Lamara. The family had three curious pets, who were full of beans: James, the little woodpecker with a big appetite; Sarah, the bonny little rabbit who never stopped talking; and Elijah, the noisy little lion cub who loved to ride his bike fast down the steep, rugged hill.

James, the little woodpecker with the big appetite, Sarah, the bonny little rabbit who never stopped talking, and Elijah, the noisy little lion cub who loved to ride his bike fast down the steep, rugged hill, were not always happy doing what they were told to do. However, James, Sarah and Elijah continued obediently to perform their duties.

One glorious day, Angela, the farmer's beautiful wife, baked an extremely delicious fruit cake. But then James, the little woodpecker with the big appetite, came along and ate it all! Not a single crumb was left.

James, the little woodpecker with the big appetite, who had eaten all the cake, started to walk quickly towards the steep, rugged hill. Sarah, the bonny little rabbit who never stopped talking, chased after James, the little woodpecker with the big appetite, who had eaten all the cake.

"Hey, James, where are you going? Come back! Come back!" she shouted.

Elijah, the noisy little lion cub who loved to ride his bike fast down the steep, rugged hill, chased after Sarah, the bonny little rabbit who never stopped talking, and James, the little woodpecker with the big appetite, who had eaten all the cake.

Angela, the farmer's beautiful wife, who baked the delicious fruit cake, chased after Elijah, Sarah and James.

They ran and they ran down the steep, rugged hill, over the narrow wooden footbridge and across the green open field, to the wide and deep flowing river.

James, the little woodpecker with the big appetite, who had eaten all the cake, jumped into the wide and deep flowing river.

Sarah, the bonny little rabbit who never stopped talking, jumped into the wide and deep flowing river after James, the little woodpecker with the big appetite, who had eaten all the cake.

Elijah, the noisy little lion cub who loved to ride his bike fast down the steep, rugged hill, jumped into the wide and deep flowing river after Sarah, the bonny little rabbit who never stopped talking, and James, the little woodpecker with the big appetite, who had eaten all the cake.

Angela, the farmer's beautiful wife, who baked the delicious fruit cake, stopped by the edge of the wide and deep flowing river. She did not know how to swim, so she stood with her hands on her hips and her eyes and mouth wide open. She watched as her three beautiful pets all happily swam away in the wide and deep flowing river.

With their heads held high, they swam fast. The water splashed bubbles all around them.

Daniel, the young farmer, heard the excitement and came running to see what was going on. He put his arm around his wife's shoulders. They stood and watched, with sad eyes, as their three beautiful pets, James, Sarah and Elijah, disappeared out of their sight towards a faraway secluded land.

James, the little woodpecker with the big appetite, who had eaten all the cake, Sarah, the bonny little rabbit who never stopped talking, and Elijah, the little lion cub who loved to ride his bike fast down the steep, rugged hill, all happily swam away to the most beautiful island far away down the magnificent river.

On a large oval wooden gate was a sign written in the colours of the rainbow. It read, 'Welcome to Logwood Lane, the Animals' Kingdom, the Land of Plenty, Where No Human Shall Ever Enter'.

"Oh my! What a marvellous day!" they whispered, almost at the same time.

James, the little woodpecker with the big appetite, who had eaten all the cake, Sarah, the bonny little rabbit who never stopped talking, and Elijah, the noisy little lion cub who loved to ride his bike fast down the steep, rugged hill, were very exhausted and almost out of breath. However, they were delighted and excited to be in such strange and beautiful surroundings.

They were greeted at the gate by Joyce, the graceful hummingbird; Esme, the beautiful little squirrel; and Jude, the gorgeous little owl. They walked slowly with James, Sarah and Elijah towards an enormous hut with a green door, where they would stay for the night.

"You are all tired. You must rest and have something to eat," said Joyce. "Tomorrow you shall see more of the landscape and the others that live here."

Then, hand in hand, Joyce, Esme and Jude elegantly glided away.

The land was cultivated with a multitude of plants. There were many trees and an amazing meadow that stretched out to meet the golden skies. There were palm trees laden with large coconuts. Banana plants with ripe bananas. Mango trees with blossoms, green mangoes and ripe mangoes. Oh, what pretty sight! Pear trees, apple trees, plum trees and many more fruit trees that they had never seen before.

The branches of the trees were bent to the ground, loaded with sweet, delicious fruit, all ready to be eaten. Oh, what heavenly beauty!

"Oh my! Bless our mama and papa! We are going to be mighty happy here," whispered James, the little woodpecker with the big appetite, who had eaten all the cake.

Sarah, the bonny little rabbit who never stopped talking, and Elijah, the noisy little lion cub who loved to ride his bike fast down the steep, rugged hill, were far too tired to utter another word. They could only nod their heads in agreement.

They entered the large hut with the green door. There they had the most delicious buffet meal they had ever eaten, and some cool coconut water too, which had been beautifully spread out for them.

Soon they were all ready to sleep. Carefully they walked into a large, warm room – a room created for travellers. Its roof was made of coconut and banana leaves; the walls were made of bamboo and fig leaves. The beds were of soft, clean cotton.

Without a word between them, James, Sarah and Elijah crept quietly into bed. They rested their heads on the big, soft pillows. They closed their eyes and in no time at all they were fast asleep and were carried away into dreamland. In dreamland they saw all the friendly animals that live in the magnificent Land of Tranquillity.

In dreamland they also met up with some friends from the farm. There were Bell, the happy donkey with long ears; Gips, the devoted sleepy old shaggy dog; and Tibs, the cheerful black-and-white cat. Oh yes, Zelda, the adorable honey-coloured puppy, was there too; she was playing delightful music on her violin. She was very, very happy indeed! There were some great spotted woodpeckers, hummingbirds, peacocks and peahens, guinea pigs and rabbits, butterflies and swarms of merry bees making delicious honey.

Later in their dream, they saw Norman, the humorous little dolphin, playing soft goodnight music on his flute for the others, to send them off into sweet sleep.

James, Sarah and Elijah slept until just before the sun rose high above the faraway steep, rugged hill. Then they heard a melodious voice. It was the voice of Franklyn, the adorable nightingale.

"Good morning, everyone. Welcome to Logwood Lane, the Land of Plenty. Lovely to see you all. Have a nice day, now!"

After a large, delicious breakfast of papayas, mangoes, roasted sweet potatoes, carrots, cabbages and some honey, James, the little woodpecker with the big appetite, who ate all the cake, Sarah, the bonny little rabbit who never stopped talking, and Elijah, the noisy little lion cub who loved to ride his bike fast down the steep, rugged hill, all set out to work.

Meanwhile, back on the farm, Daniel, the young farmer, and Angela, his beautiful wife, who baked the delicious fruit cake, sadly walked back across the green open field, over the narrow wooden footbridge and up the steep, rugged hill to their home.

Lamara, their graceful, magical daughter, ran to meet them, but was surprised that her mama and papa looked so sad.

She looked up at them and asked, "Mama, Papa, what is wrong? Why are you so sad?"

"They are gone! James, Sarah and Elijah – all gone. They swam away down the river, and they won't be coming back," said her mama in a low voice. "That is why we are so sad, my dear child."

"Mama, don't worry – they will be fine. I can go and visit them."

"No, my darling, humans are not allowed on the island where I suspect they have gone, and in any case the river is far too wide for you to get across," said her Mama.

"I know where you mean, Mama. I have read all about that lovely island, and I know the animals that live there are very happy. Mama, Papa, please come with me, to my magical playhouse."

She held their hands and off they went to Lamara's magical playhouse. It was the most beautiful playhouse they had ever seen. It was grand and amazingly pretty, clean, warm and colourful – like a palace, gallery and library all in one. A little playhouse fit for the Queen of England!

There were lots of watercolour paintings on the walls and some pottery on display. There were bookshelves filled with all kinds of books! Books about dancing fairies, books about dragons breathing fire, books about princes and princesses with crowns on their heads, and books about humans climbing up to the moon. Best of all was a well-read book about the animals' kingdom.

"You are a clever girl!" said her mama.

In Lamara's playhouse there was a large wooden table and four wooden chairs placed in the middle of the room. Lamara, James, Sarah and Elijah would sit there and read every evening when they were not chasing away cheeky rats and sly foxes from the chicken house.

"Mama, Papa, look," said Lamara. "I will close my eyes and say my magic words."

"Be careful, darling. Mind you don't turn into a frog!" said her papa, smiling at her.

"Or you might turn into a snake. I don't like snakes at all," said her mama.

Lamara closed her eyes and said the magic words: "Oh, my wise one from the mountain, you mighty magical one, please turn me into a kind, beautiful fairy."

And there she was, in a flash, all dressed up like a real fairy.

"See!" she declared with glee. Then she spoke magic words once more: "Oh, my wise one from the mountain, you mighty magical one, please turn me back into my human self."

With a flash of soft light, she was back to her old self.

"Thank you, my wise one," she said.

"Thank goodness for that!" declared her mama.

"Now then, let us bake some lovely fruit cakes for James, Sarah and Elijah," announced Lamara.

And so they did.

Early the next morning, Lamara picked up a large picnic basket filled with lots of small delicious fruit cakes of all shapes, sizes and colours and some books for them to read in the evening. Oh yes – read to be wise!

She closed her eyes and said the magic words: "Oh, my wise one from the mountain, you mighty magical one, please take me to the gate of the animals' kingdom."

And in seconds she was a beautiful fairy, standing at the gate of the animals' kingdom, where no human was ever allowed to enter.

"James, Sarah, Elijah," she called as loudly as she could.

They recognized her voice and merrily they all came running to greet her.

"Look! Look! I brought lots of delicious fruit cakes for you!" she said with excitement.

With bright eyes they all said, "Thank you, our loveable Lamara," while they looked greedily into the basket of yummy fruit cakes.

"Are you all glad to be here in this land of perfection?" asked Lamara.

"Yes, we are truly glad to be here in this scrumptious, plentiful and peaceful land, and we love you lots," they answered.

"Jolly good," she said. "I am truly happy for you all, and I love you too."

After a long cheerful chat and hugs, it was time for Lamara to go back home.

She waved to them and said, "Goodbye, my lovely ones. Be happy." Then she closed her eyes and spoke the magic words: "Oh, you wise one from the mountain, you mighty magical one, please take me home."

In no time at all she was home, with good news for her papa and her beautiful mama. Lamara told her mama and papa that James, Sarah and Elijah were well and very merry.

"We are happy now – very happy indeed – to know that our beautiful pets, James, Sarah and Elijah, are all truly well and merry. Yes, let them live in peace," said her mama. "And you, our dearest, amazing daughter. We love you very, very much," they declared with bright eyes.

Then they hugged her tightly and gave her lots of kisses.

In the meantime, James, the little woodpecker with the big appetite, Sarah, the bonny little rabbit who never stopped talking, and Elijah, the noisy little lion cub, were busy at work, building themselves the most beautiful house you have ever seen. The house resembled Noah's Ark. The colour was of soft, warm green. It overlooked the wide and deep flowing river.

"We name this house UNITY," shouted James, Sarah and Elijah.

And a very fine house it was too! There was a beautiful kitchen and a large pantry where an abundance of grains and seeds and plenty of extremely delicious cakes and cookies were stored.

The cakes and cookies were of different shapes and sizes. Some were round with red and white dots. Some were squares with icing on the top. There were also some pink and blue triangles and some half-moon ones too, which they shared with their friends and neighbours.

Every Sunday and on Christmas Day, Lamara and her mama and papa would slowly walk down the steep, rugged hill, over the narrow wooden footbridge and across the green open field, to the wide and deep flowing river. Lamara would stand by the edge of the river with the large picnic basket filled with lots of small delicious fruit cakes.

As usual she closed her eyes and said the magic words: "Oh, you wise one from the mountain, you mighty magical one, please take me to the gate of the animals' kingdom." And in a flash she was standing at the gate, calling, "James, Sarah, Elijah, I'm here!"

And they all happily came running to meet her.

As usual she gave them lots of hugs and kisses.

"Oh, James, your feathers are so soft," she said as she gently brushed her hand over his wings. "And you, Sarah – what bright eyes! Oh, Elijah, you are growing so big and strong!"

And they all laughed joyfully.

"I love you all," Lamara said. "Mama and Papa love you very much and want you all to be very happy."

"Thank you, our loveable Lamara. We love you all," they answered.

Once more it was time to say her goodbyes: "Goodbye, James; goodbye, Sarah; goodbye, Elijah; goodbye, everyone. See you," she said. Then she closed her eyes and said the magic words: "Oh, you wise one from the mountain, you mighty magical one, please take me home."

And in a flash she was gone.

In the evenings, James, Sarah, Elijah and their friends all sat on their large veranda overlooking the wide and deep flowing river. They would watch the setting of the glorious sun wishing them goodnight and slowly disappearing out of their sight. Later they would read books and talk about their life on the farm.

"This is the best life for us. We work together. We are equal in this beautiful land of peace and plenty – of delicious food too," said James, the little woodpecker.

"This life is wonderful. We work, talk, eat and have sweet sleep when we want, and we have time to see the stars and the rising of the glorious full moon. Yes, we are in paradise," shouted Sarah, the bonny little rabbit.

"It was good on the farm, but this place is the Land of Plenty," shouted Elijah, the noisy little lion cub.

"Hooray!" they all shouted with laughter.

Goodness gracious me! I nearly forgot to tell you what James, Sarah and Elijah had been getting up to.

Oh yes, James, the little woodpecker with the big appetite, who had eaten all the cake, Sarah, the bonny little rabbit who never stopped talking, and Elijah, the noisy little lion cub who loved to ride his bike fast down the steep, rugged hill, all attended the University of Aspiration, in Logwood Lane, the Land of Plenty, 'where no human shall ever enter'.

At the University of Aspiration James is studying 'food for the soul and body'. Sarah is studying 'how to talk forever and never get tired'. And Elijah is studying 'how to ride a bike and never fall off'.

Oh yes, curiosity means knowledge! Knowledge means wealth!

Let them never stop learning. Young ladies and gentlemen, a good education is a friend forever.

And they all lived happily, forever and ever.